The Night Before Christmas

Clement C. Moore
Illustrated by Becky Kelly

Andrews McMeel Publishing, LLC
Kansas City

07 08 09 10 11 EPB 10 9 8 7 6 5 4 3 2

ISBN-13: 978-0-7407-6064-8
ISBN-10: 0-7407-6064-5

www.beckykelly.com
www.andrewsmcmeel.com

for my father,
Robert L. Wilson

Twas the night before Christmas,
when all through the house
Not a creature was stirring,
not even a mouse;

The stockings were hung
by the chimney with care
In hopes that St. Nicholas
soon would be there;

he children were nestled
all snug in their beds,
While visions of sugar-plums
danced in their heads;

And mamma in her kerchief,
and I in my cap,
Had just settled our brains
for a long winter's nap,

When out on the lawn
there arose such a clatter,
I sprang from my bed
to see what was the matter.

Away to the window
I flew like a flash,
Tore open the shutters
and threw up the sash.

The moon on the breast
of the new-fallen snow
Gave the lustre of mid-day
to objects below,

When, what to my wondering
eyes should appear,
But a miniature sleigh,
and eight tiny reindeer,

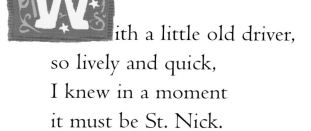

ith a little old driver,
so lively and quick,
I knew in a moment
it must be St. Nick.

More rapid than eagles
his coursers they came,
And he whistled, and shouted,
and called them by name:

ow, Dasher! now, Dancer!
now, Prancer and Vixen!
On, Comet! on, Cupid!
on, Donder and Blitzen!

To the top of the porch!
to the top of the wall!
Now dash away! dash away!
dash away all!"

As dry leaves that before
the wild hurricane fly,
When they meet with an obstacle,
mount to the sky;

So up to the house-top
the coursers they flew,
With the sleigh full of toys,
and St. Nicholas too.

And then, in a twinkling,
I heard on the roof
The prancing and pawing
of each little hoof.

As I drew in my head,
and was turning around,
Down the chimney St. Nicholas
came with a bound.

He was dressed all in fur,
from his head to his foot,
And his clothes were all tarnished
with ashes and soot;

A bundle of toys
he had flung on his back,
And he looked like a peddler
just opening his pack.

His eyes, how they twinkled!
his dimples, how merry!
His cheeks were like roses,
his nose like a cherry!

His droll little mouth
was drawn up like a bow,
And the beard on his chin
was as white as the snow;

The stump of a pipe
he held tight in his teeth,
And the smoke it encircled
his head like a wreath;

He had a broad face
and a little round belly,
That shook when he laughed,
like a bowl full of jelly.

He was chubby and plump,
a right jolly old elf,
And I laughed when I saw him
in spite of myself;

A wink of his eye
and a twist of his head,
Soon gave me to know
I had nothing to dread.

He spoke not a word,
but went straight to his work,
And filled all the stockings;
then turned with a jerk,

And laying his finger
aside of his nose,
And giving a nod,
up the chimney he rose.

He sprang to his sleigh,
to his team gave a whistle,
And away they all flew
like the down of a thistle.

But I heard him exclaim
ere he drove out of sight,

erry Christmas to all,

and to all a good-night!

To: Aiden
From: Mommy and
Daddy
Merry Christmas!!
12-25-07